THE SERPENT-BEARER

&

THE PRINCE

OF

STARS

A SHORT STORY OF DEMONS & STARLIGHT

☼

STORY BY
C. S. Johnson

ART BY
Eko Bambang

C. S. JOHNSON

Ebook ISBN: 9781948464185
Paperback ISBN: 9781948464192

Story originally published in *Spectacular Tales 2: The Science Fiction and Fantasy Collection (The Indie Collaboration Presents Book 10)*, available online as an ebook (ASIN: B016S179EE). The story exists in the world of The Starlight Chronicles, an epic fantasy adventure series by C. S. Johnson.

Artistry for the comics provided by Eko Bambang.

Dedicated with much love to my (Almost) Famous Readers. I may have days where I walk in darkness, but your kindness proves I will never walk alone so long as you are with me.

C. S. JOHNSON

THE HEAVENS WERE ALIGHT WITH FESTIVE FIRE AND A CHEERING CROWD

MANY HAD ARRIVED TO THE KINGDOM HALL'S CELEBRATION SINGING, OVERFLOWING WITH HAPPINESS AND JOY, AND THE OTHERS WERE STILL POURING IN.

TAP TAP

YOU'RE NOT ALONE...

I'M HERE

I MIGHT HAVE BEEN STUPID IN TAKING YOU, BUT I WOULD HAVE BEEN EVEN MORE STUPID TO SAY NO TO THE PRINCE OF STARS

YOU'VE TALKED TO THE PRINCE OF STARS, OPHIUCHUS? I'M SUR-PRISED YOU WOULD TELL SUCH A STORY.

IT'S NOT LIKE YOU TO ASSERT YOUR CLAIM TO FAME; AT LEAST, IT HASN'T BEEN, SINCE YOU'VE GOTTEN THAT SERPENT

WHICH I SEE YOU STILL HAVE

NAGA IS UNDER MY CARE UNTIL THE PRINCE WANTS HIM BACK

I'M SURE, IT DOESN'T SEEM LIKE THE PRINCE IS THE KIND OF PERSON TO GIVE ONE A DUTY AS DEMANDING AND CRUEL AS THIS ONE. AFTER ALL, HE'S ONLY ASKED ME TO HELP WITH THE ZODIAC DUTIES ONCE EVERY YEAR ON EARTH. YOU REALLY OUGHT TO THINK ABOUT GETTING RID OF NAGA ON YOUR OWN, IF YOU ARE NOT SO ATTACHED TO HIM

OPHIUCHUS AND I ARE PRETTY CLOSE

RIGHT, OPHIU-CHUS?

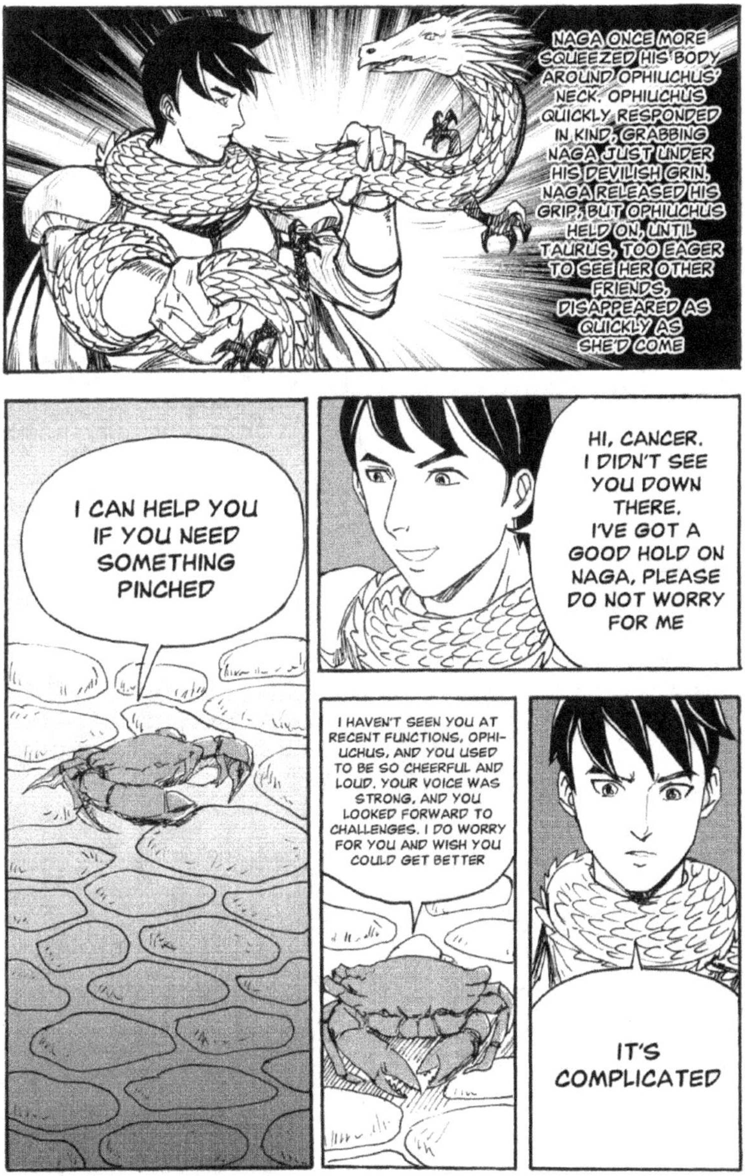

NAGA ONCE MORE SQUEEZED HIS BODY AROUND OPHIUCHUS' NECK. OPHIUCHUS QUICKLY RESPONDED IN KIND, GRABBING NAGA JUST UNDER HIS DEVILISH GRIN. NAGA RELEASED HIS GRIP, BUT OPHIUCHUS HELD ON, UNTIL TAURUS, TOO EAGER TO SEE HER OTHER FRIENDS, DISAPPEARED AS QUICKLY AS SHE'D COME

I CAN HELP YOU IF YOU NEED SOMETHING PINCHED

HI, CANCER. I DIDN'T SEE YOU DOWN THERE. I'VE GOT A GOOD HOLD ON NAGA, PLEASE DO NOT WORRY FOR ME

I HAVEN'T SEEN YOU AT RECENT FUNCTIONS, OPHI-UCHUS, AND YOU USED TO BE SO CHEERFUL AND LOUD. YOUR VOICE WAS STRONG, AND YOU LOOKED FORWARD TO CHALLENGES. I DO WORRY FOR YOU AND WISH YOU COULD GET BETTER

IT'S COMPLICATED

I JUST WANT TO SEE YOU HAPPY. YOU ALWAYS SEEM SO LONELY AND SAD NOW. IT'S ALMOST LIKE YOU'VE GIVEN UP ON BEING HAPPY OR HAVING SOMETHING WORTH HAVING

I HAVE THE SAME AS YOU - A DUTY TO OUR PRINCE. YOUR CONCERN IS MISPLACED, FRIEND

I'M NOT SO SURE. I THINK YOU'RE LYING TO YOURSELF. YOU NEED TO GET OVER THIS COMPLEX OF YOURS, OPHIUCHUS. YOU'RE ONLY HURTING YOURSELF AND THE PEOPLE YOU CARE ABOUT BY CLINGING TO IT

HE SEEMS NICE. HE WAS THE ONE WHO USED TO COME AND VISIT US, DIDN'T HE ?

HAA...

HA... HAA...

YES !

THE PRINCE WAS PROBABLY TESTING YOU, TO SEE IF YOUR PRIDE WOULD CAVE BEFORE HE HAS CORRECT YOU. IT WAS PROBABLY A PUNISHMENT, SINCE YOU WERE SO INSISTENT THAT WE KEEP YOU IN THE ZODIAC FAMILY.

YES, I DON'T RECALL CETAN GIVING US SO MUCH TROUBLE WHEN WE TALKED ABOUT MAKING IT A BAND OF TWELVE

HE WAS FINE WITH BEING EXCLUDED. OF COURSE, HE'S MUCH HAPPIER AND MUCH MORE UPBEAT THAN YOU ARE. IN FACT, I WAS FINE WITH KEEPING HIM IN THE ZODIAC. PROBABLY BECAUSE HE DIDN'T TRY TO CUT INTO MY TIME.

CAPRICORN WAS DEFINITELY AMBITIOUS. OPHIUCHUS KNEW. SHE HAD NOT BEEN PLEASED AT HIS INTENT TO STAY IN THE ZODIAC CONSTELLATION, ESPECIALLY AFTER SHE HAD PLEADED WITH THE PRINCE HIMSELF OVER THE MATTER

I KNOW YOU LIKE WATCHING OVER EARTH, CAPRICORN

BUT THERE WAS NOTHING ABOUT WANTING TO BE A PART OF THE FAMILY, LIKE I RIGHTFULLY AM. AND CETAN HAS THE SAME PRIVILEGE AS I DO. EVEN IF WE ARE NOT AS POWERFUL NOR AS CENTRAL TO POLARIS AS YOU

OPHIUCHUS FELT THE HEAT RISE IN HIS CHEEKS, ANGRY AND FRUSTRATED AT SO MANY THINGS ALL AT ONCE. HE THOUGHT ABOUT TRYING TO EXPLAIN EVERYTHING, ALL OVERALL AGAIN.

BUT A COUPLE OF OTHER STARS CAUGHT HIS ATTENTION, THEY WERE LAUGHING AND POINTING AT HIM FROM ACROSS THE HALL

HUA.. HAHAHAH...

YOU WERE BROUGHT HERE FROM THE EARTH, SNAKE, WHILE OPHIUCHUS WAS BORN OF THE NIGHT. WHY WOULD WE ASSUME YOU ARE STRONGER THAN OPHIUCHUS?

I MIGHT HAVE COME FROM EARTH, BUT I HAVE DEATH IN ME. EVEN YOU ARE NOT IMMUNE TO DEATH.

THE TWINS EXCHANGED LOOKS AND THEN, QUIETLY AND RESPECTFULLY, EXCUSED THEMSELVES

WE WISH YOU THE BEST, OPHIUCHUS !

GOOD LUCK IN GETTING BETTER

LET'S GO !!

OOH, BUT THE PARTY HAS ONLY JUST BEGUN

I DON'T CARE. I'D BEEN ASKED TO COME BY THE PRINCE, AND THAT'S WHAT I DID.

HE DIDN'T TELL ME HOW LONG TO STAY HERE, AND I'LL DO AS I PLEASE FOR ONCE. THAT MIGHT EVEN HELP; MANY HERE THINK I AM INCAPABLE OF DOING THAT WHEN IT COMES TO KEEPING YOU IN LINE. IT WILL BE GOOD OF ME TO SHOW THEM I AM STILL STRONG AND STILL CAPABLE OF CHOOSING TO DO WHAT MAKES ME HAPPY.

GOOD FOR YOU. TAKE A STAND FOR YOURSELF. I MEAN, REALLY, AFTER ALL THIS TIME, THE PRINCE HAS JUST LEFT ME WITH YOU, AND DIDN'T TELL YOU ANYTHING ABOUT HOW LONG IT WOULD BE, OR EVEN REALLY WHY HE GAVE ME TO YOU. YOU JUST CAN'T TRUST SOMEONE WHO HIDES THE TRUTH OF THESE SORTS OF THINGS

OPHIUCHUS FELT HIS TONGUE GO DRY AT THE THOUGHT OF CAPRICORN'S WORDS. COULD NAGA HAVE BEEN A PUNISHMENT ?

I DIDN'T SAY THAT. I'VE BEEND A GOOD SERVANT TO MY MASTER, AND I WILL CONTINUE TO DO WHAT IS RIGHT.

EVEN WHEN I'VE DONE MY VERY WORST TO KEEP YOU UNHAPPY ?. I'M HONORED, I REALLY AM. THIS IS PERFECT ! A WILLING VICTIM IS ALWAYS THE BEST KIND OF VICTIM

I'M NOT A VICTIM !

I CHOSE TO WATCH OVER YOU !

HILARIOUS ! NOT JUST A VICTIM OF HIS PRINCE, BUT OF HIS OWN REASONING, TOO. SEE ? IT IS AS I TOLD YOU ERLIER. YOU'RE STUPID

AND YOU'RE UNHAPPY, AND SUFFERING, AND IGNORED BY ALL YOUR SOCALLED FRIENDS, AND YOUR SO-CALLED BRETHREN OF THE ZODIAC. EVEN THE ONES WHO OFFERED TO HELP YOU OUT AT FIRST, AND EVEN THE ONES WHO HAVE ONLY BEEN WISHING FOR YOU TO BE RID OF ME

I CAN TAKE CARE OF YOU, NAGA, AND I HAVE DONE SO FOR MILLENNIA

YOU'RE WEAK, AND I ONLY GROW STRONGER AS YOU FADE. WE HAVE EQUAL POWER, BUT NOT EQUAL PURPOSE. I JUST HAVE TO WEAR YOU DOWN, AND MAKE YOU GIVE UP; YOU CAN HATE ME OR LOVE ME OR JUST TOLERATE ME, BUT YOU'LL NEVER BE ABLE TO GET ME TO STOP FIGHTING YOU

IT IS JUST AS I TOLD THE OTHERS: DEATH RESIDES IN ME, AND ALL OF LIFE IS JUST AN ATTEMPT TO KEEP DEATH AT BAY. AND YOU WILL NOT SUCCEED. EVEN IF I GO OUT ALONG WITH YOU, I WILL HAVE THE FINAL VICTORY IN THE END

OPHIUCHUS STOPPED AND FELT THE FULL WEIGHT AND MEANING OF NAGA'S WORDS. HE ALMOST SHUTTERED, AS HE REALIZED NAGA HAD SOLID ARGUMENTS AGAINST HIM. IT WAS POSSIBLE NAGA WOULD LEAVE HIM TO DEATH, THAT NAGA WOULD DESTROY HIS LIGHT AND HIS LIFE.

OPHIUCHUS, WE COULD MAKE A VERY GOOD PARTNERSHIP

I CAN'T DISOBEY THE PRINCE OF STARS ANY MORE THAN YOU COULD—HE RULES OVER THE EARTH AS EASILY AS HE DOES THE STARS AND ANGELS BUT THERE'S NO NEED FOR US TO BE FIGHTING THE WHOLE TIME WE'RE PUT TOGETHER, RIGHT? CAN'T YOU THINK OF SOME THINGS WE'VE AGREED ON IN THE PAST?

NO. YOU ALWAYS GO AGAINST ME

WELL, YOU'RE DOING THAT JUST NOW

JUST THINK ABOUT IT, WE DON'T HAVE TO BE ENEMIES, HERE, DO WE? THAT'S THE ONLY REASON. I AM MAKING YOUR LIFE HARD, ISN'T IT? BECAUSE YOU'RE LETTING ME, AND BECAUSE YOU THINK I'M THE ENEMY. THE PRINCE NEVER SAID ANYTHING ABOUT THAT.

OPHIUCHUS DID NOT ANSWER

HE THOUGHT IT OVER, NAGA, AS MUCH AS HE HATED TO ADMIT IT, HAD A POINT. HE DIDN'T HAVE TO MAKE HIM AN ENEMY. THE PRINCE WAS THE ONE WHO SAW NAGA AS DANGEROUS, AS A PROBLEM. OPHIUCHUS COULD PROBABLY GET ALONG WELL WITH NAGA. AFTER ALL THE TIME THEY'D BEEN TOGETHER, IS WAS SIMILAR TO WHAT HE SUSPECTED A HUMAN FELT ABOUT HIS SHADOW; IT WAS A QUIET, DARK KIND OF COMFORTABLE FAMILIARITY, AND IT WAS NOT DESIRABLE, PERHAPS, BUT IT WAS THERE, AND THERE WAS NO GETTING RID OF IT.

HE THOUGHT OF ALL HIS FRIENDS WHO HAD WATCHED HIM SUFFER WITH NAGA SUFFOCATING HIM, AND THE PAIN – OH, THE MEMORIES OF THE PAIN HAD BEEN THE WORST. MEMORIES OF NAGA SQUEEZING HIM, SNIPING AT HIM, HISSING AT HIM, ALL WHILE THE EARTH KEPT GOING AROUND ITS SUN, AND THE OTHER ZODIAC EITHER IGNORED HIM OR EVENTUALLY LEFT HIM TO SUFFER, UNABLE OR UNWILLING TO ARGUE WITH HIM OR DEAL WITH HIM. IT WAS ONLY AS THEY CAME UPON OPHIUCHUS' HOME– A BRIGHT AND SHINING PALACE, MADE OF THE PUREST TRANSPARENT GOLD, THAT HIS THOUGHTS WERE OVERTAKEN

LORD ? WHAT ARE YOU DOING HERE ?

I WAS JUST THERE, I DID NOT DISOBEY YOU

WHAT AM I DOING HERE? SHOULDN'T THE QUESTION BE, WHAT ARE YOU DOING HERE? I INVITED YOU TO COME TO MY PARTY

NO, YOU DID NOT, BUT IT IS EARLY. THE PARTY IS NOT OVER. I THOUGHT IT BEST TO LEAVE

SUCH SORROW. IT IS NEVER EASY, BEARING A BURDEN. AND IT IS HARDER YET TO BEAR ONE WHICH NO ONE UNDERSTANDS.

OPHIUCHUS STEPPED BACK

I CHOSE THIS, I UNDERSTAND IT IS MUCH HARDER THAN I THOUGHT IT WOULD BE. I DIDN'T REALIZE JUST WHAT YOU WERE ASKING OF ME. I DON'T THINK I AM THE RIGHT ONE TO LOOK AFTER NAGA ANYMORE

I'M NOT STRONG ENOUGH TO CARRY ON FOR MUCH LONGER, AND I JUST WANT TO BE HAPPY AGAIN, AND TO HAVE THE RESPECT OF THE OTHERS. PLEASE, MY LORD, PLEASE TAKE THIS PAIN FROM ME, AND FORGIVE ME FOR BEING SO WEAK

YOU'VE CARRIED THIS FOR SO LONG. YOU ARE STRONGER THAN YOU REALIZE. THERE IS NO NEED FOR APOLOGY. OPHIUCHUS, DO YOU KNOW THE REASON I INVITED YOU TO THE PARTY TONIGHT?

NO, LORD

TONIGHT IS A SPECIAL NIGHT; TONIGHT, ONE OF MY PROMISES IS GOING TO BE FULFILLED. I HAVE NEED FOR NAGA. I AM GOING TO RELEASE HIM BACK DOWN TO EARTH, BECAUSE THE TIME HAS COME FOR HIS HEAD TO BE CRUSHED BY THE HEEL HE TRIED TO POISON

NAGA, STILL SILENT, FELL LIMP AROUND HIS BODY

HE WILL BE PUNISHED?

DO YOU THINK IT IS WRONG TO PUNISH HIM?

NAGA LAY ACROSS HIS ARMS, STILL ALIVE AND WARM. OPHIUCHUS FELT ALL THE BURDEN OF ALL THE LONG YEARS RETREAT, AND THE SPIRIT INSIDE OF HIM GREW. HIS MUSCLE WERE TAUT, AND HIS BODY, NOW COMPLETELY UPRIGHT, AND HE FELT ALL HIS WORLD WITHIN HIM AND AROUND HIM SWELL WITH HAPPINESS AND GOODNESS.

FOR A WHILE, I THOUGHT HE WOULD BE NOTHING BUT TROUBLE. I WAS DOING SOMETHING FOR YOU TO SHOW YOU I COULD BE OF HELP TO YOU. BUT I KNOW FROM NAGA I AM NOT ABLE TO HELP YOU AS MUCH AS I'D LIKE, THAT I'M NOT NEEDED FOR YOUR WORK TO GET DONE. I THINK OF ALL THE THINGS HE HAS PUT ME THROUGH, AND ALL THE THINGS I HAVE BEEN THROUGH AS A RESULT. HE TRIED TO CALL HIMSELF MY FRIEND, BUT HE IS NO ONE'S FRIEND

HE HAS DONE NOTHING BUT TRY TO DISSUADE ME FROM FOLLOWING YOU. HE BRINGS NOTHING BUT DIVISION BETWEEN ME AND MY FRIENDS AND FAMILY. HE IS MY ENEMY.

OPHIUCHUS BLINKED, AS THOUGH HEARING IS FOR THE FIRST TIME FROM HIS OWN WORDS MADE IT MORE REAL AND CLEARER THAN EVEN BEFORE

HE IS MY ENEMY

SO WHAT IS YOUR ANSWER ?

....

YOUR WILL SHOULD BE DONE. HE HAS BROUGHT BOTH GOOD AND BAD INTO MY LIFE; YOU WILL JUDGE HIM ACCORDING TO WHAT IS RIGHT

LET'S GO BACK TO THE PARTY AND GIVE HIM A PROPER SEND OFF

OPHIUCHUS SMILED AS NAGA, HIS MOUTH STILL SEALED SHUT, COULD ONLY SCOWL. ALL OD HIS TROUBLE, ALL OF OPHIUCHUS' PAIN AND LONG-SUFFERING, ALL OF IT SUDDENLY SEEMED WORTH IT, TO GET TO THIS MOMENT.

AUTHOR'S NOTE

Dear Reader,

The question of evil—or perhaps more accurately, the problem of evil—often haunts a lot of people, and I include myself in that from time to time. The thing I've always thought about evil which made it so difficult to handle was that it was always so capable of adaptation. If you think about it, this make sense, since goodness, in its purest form, does not need to adapt; once evil takes goodness and twists it, it can never go back to being "good," again.

So with all this in mind, I look at the world and wonder why there is such suffering and why it seems as though evil goes unchecked. It is a daunting question, that's for sure. But it's not for the cynic to stay skeptical, just as it's not up to the faithful to remain flippant. While I trust in something greater than evil and its power, and I know that it is only a matter of time before the world's pain is resolved, I still find myself questioning myself and my Prince, and I also sometimes stumble into a den full of doubters and discouragers.

In this story, Ophiuchus is given a task—a burden to bear—and it is much more difficult than it seems. He is asked to be the one who bears the serpent, who holds him fast. In many ways, it seems like an easy thing. But as the story shows, some serpents are more crafty than we would like to admit, and the wounds they inflict are more damaging than we notice.

I wanted to try to make sense of my own pain. My own dragon, my depression, has weighed itself around my neck and on my back quite often. I do wonder why this burden was given to me to bear, but even more so, I am called to take up my cross and carry it, as I follow my lord. And that means my Naga will have a home until my Prince comes and puts him in his proper place. Sometimes, I am forgetful, and I need the reminder that my dragon, my demon, is not my friend. I need the reminder that other people can discourage me even more often than they can encourage me, and I need to hold firm to the truth if I am going to stay the course I'm called to follow.

I might have to go through hell, but I must keep my eyes on heaven. And that goes for you, too; I pray you will find the courage, the strength, and the resolve to do what you need to do, even if it is just one choice at a time.

Until We Meet Again,

C. S. Johnson

OTHER WORKS BY THE AUTHOR

The Starlight Chronicles, by C. S. Johnson

Everyone has a set of beliefs that sets them apart from others.

When a meteorite strikes the heart of Apollo City, sixteen-year-old Hamilton Dinger finds all of his beliefs—mainly in himself—unable to stand against the reality of his supernatural powers. Tensions increase as the meteorite unlocks the Seven Deadly Sinisters, and their leader, Orpheus, and they begin to attack the city's citizens. With Elysian, a changeling dragon, and Starry Knight, a beautiful but dangerous warrior, Hamilton must overcome his inner struggles, seal away the bad guys, and still finish his homework. Join Hamilton throughout this seven-book series as he becomes the superhero Wingdinger and sets out to save the day ... and the world.

Once Upon a Princess, by C. S. Johnson

Life is unfair, even for princesses.

When Rose—officially Princess Aurora Rosemarie—was born, she was cursed by Magdalina, the wicked rulers of the fairies. Under her curse, Rose is destined to prick her finger and die on her eighteenth birthday. When Rose learns of her curse, she sets out to do what she can to break it. Along for the ride are her friends Theo, raised in the church, but in search of his own vengeance; Mary, a young fairy who has watched over Rose since she was little; and Ethan and Sophia, a pair of siblings with a troubled past.

Can Rose find a way to break her curse and save herself? Find out in this four-part novella series, inspired by *Sleeping Beauty*.

The Divine Space Pirates, by C. S. Johnson

If survival is all that matters, does truth still make a difference?

There is nothing Aerie St. Cloud wants more than her family unit's love—until she is accidentally captured by the fearsome space pirate, Captain Chainsword, and she is stuck on his pirated starship, the *Perdition*. Aerie soon realizes the difference that the truth does make, as she finds herself falling in love with the tragic space pirate captain. Can her love help bridge the gap between her worlds? Or will it just lead to more destruction?

MORE BOOKS ON THE WAY!

SIGN UP FOR THE MAILING LIST!

Get emails full of updates and insights, and possible prizes when you sign up for the mailing list!

Sign up at https://www.csjohnson.me

Thank you for reading!
Please leave a review for this book and let others know what you think!